MARTIAN INVASION
Virgil Defeats the Hood

Sally Byford

CARLTON
BOOKS

The Hood had a plan to uncover International Rescue's secrets. He travelled to the desert in disguise to work on a film called *Martian Invasion.*

In the film the Martians had to bomb a cave where two police officers were hiding. The Hood planned to cause a terrible accident so that International Rescue would have to be called out.

Then he'd film them in action and sell their secrets to the mysterious General X.

First, the Hood needed help from his half-brother, Kyrano, who worked for International Rescue. In his temple, he used magic to get Kyrano in his power.

"Go to Thunderbird 1," the Hood ordered Kyrano, "and switch off the automatic camera detector."

So, while Kyrano was under the Hood's spell, he crept over to Thunderbird 1 and switched off the detector. Now the Hood would be able to film the aircraft without Scott knowing.

When the filming started, the two actors playing police officers hid in a cave and the Martians bombed them. Everyone was shocked by the size of the explosion. They did not know that the Hood had been at work. The cave started to collapse and water poured in.

"We'd better call International Rescue," said the Hood.

Mr Goldheimer, the director, called for help. "Two of the actors are trapped," he told Jeff Tracy. "Please come quickly!"

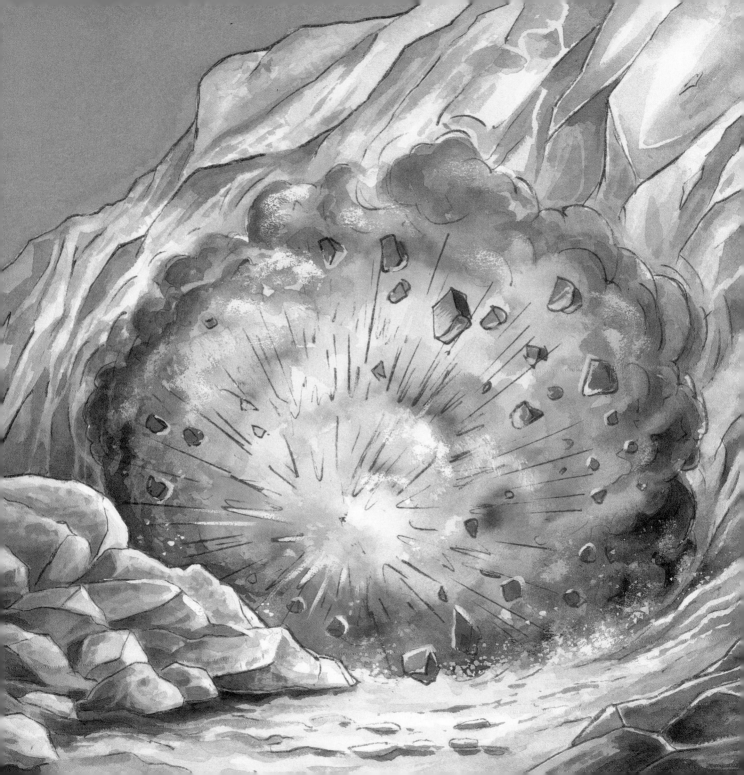

Scott and Virgil soon arrived in Thunderbirds 1 and 2. As soon as they saw what had happened, Virgil released the Excavator and started drilling through the rocks that blocked the cave's entrance.

Meanwhile the Hood was secretly filming every detail of International Rescue's equipment.

"My plan is working perfectly," he laughed.

Inside the cave, the two actors playing the police officers were very scared. They clung to the rocks, but the water was rising fast. Suddenly they heard Scott's voice on the radio.

"Stay calm," he said. "When I give the word, jump into the water. The pressure will carry you out through the hole we have drilled in the side of the mountain. Now, jump!"

The men jumped. They knew it was their only chance.

The two actors shot out of the hole just before the cave roof collapsed. They were wet and shivering, but they were safe. The rescue had been a success.

Scott was about to leave in Thunderbird 1 when Mr Goldheimer rushed up and took a photograph of him.

The camera detector didn't sound its alarm. Scott was puzzled.

"It must be switched off," he said. "Someone could have taken a film of the whole rescue."

Suddenly, they heard a Jeep speeding away. Mr Goldheimer looked through his binoculars. It was the Hood, without his disguise.

"That man's stolen a reel of film," he cried.

Scott knew it could be a film of the rescue. He chased after the Hood in Thunderbird 1, but the Jeep vanished into a tunnel.

The Hood called General X.

"I'll deliver the film as soon as I have escaped from International Rescue," he said.

Scott stopped outside the tunnel and contacted his father.

"There are two entrances to that tunnel, Scott," said Jeff. "I'll send Virgil in Thunderbird 2 to take your place. You must go to the other entrance."

"I'm on my way, father," said Scott.

"Don't let that film get away," said Jeff. "If our secrets are discovered, it will be the end of International Rescue."

As soon as Scott had left to find the other entrance, the Hood made his escape. Virgil arrived just in time to see him driving away at top speed. Quickly, he contacted his father.

"Do everything you can to stop him, Virgil," said Jeff. "We've got to get that film."

Virgil bombed the mountains at the side of the road. There was a landslide and the Hood's Jeep was trapped.

The Hood jumped out of his Jeep and ran off. He hadn't gone far when he saw an empty plane. "Perfect!" he said, and he climbed in and took off.

He called General X on his radio to tell him that he had managed to escape from International Rescue and would soon be handing over the film. But then he realized that there was something wrong with the plane. It was dropping towards the ground because the controls were not working properly.

Scott was following close behind.

At last the Hood saw General X's villa ahead, but by now he couldn't control the plane at all. Scott watched as it crashed into the front of the villa. This was the end of the Hood's evil plan.

Scott contacted his father. "The film couldn't have survived that smash," he said.

"Well done," said Jeff. "Thanks to you and Virgil the Hood has been beaten and International Rescue's secrets are safe. This mission is now complete."

THIS IS A CARLTON BOOK

Published by Carlton Books Limited 2000
20 Mortimer Street
London W1N 7RD

2 4 6 8 10 9 7 5 3

A CIP catalogue for this book is available from the British Library.

ISBN 1 84222 100 0

Illustrations by County Studio
Language consultant: Betty Root, formerly director of
Reading Centre, The University of Reading
Project editor: Lesley Levene
Production: Garry Lewis

Printed in Italy